Rosie Becomes a Warrior

A story to empower children with type 1 diabetes to live their happiest lives.

WRITTEN & ILLUSTRATED BY
JULIA FLAHERTY

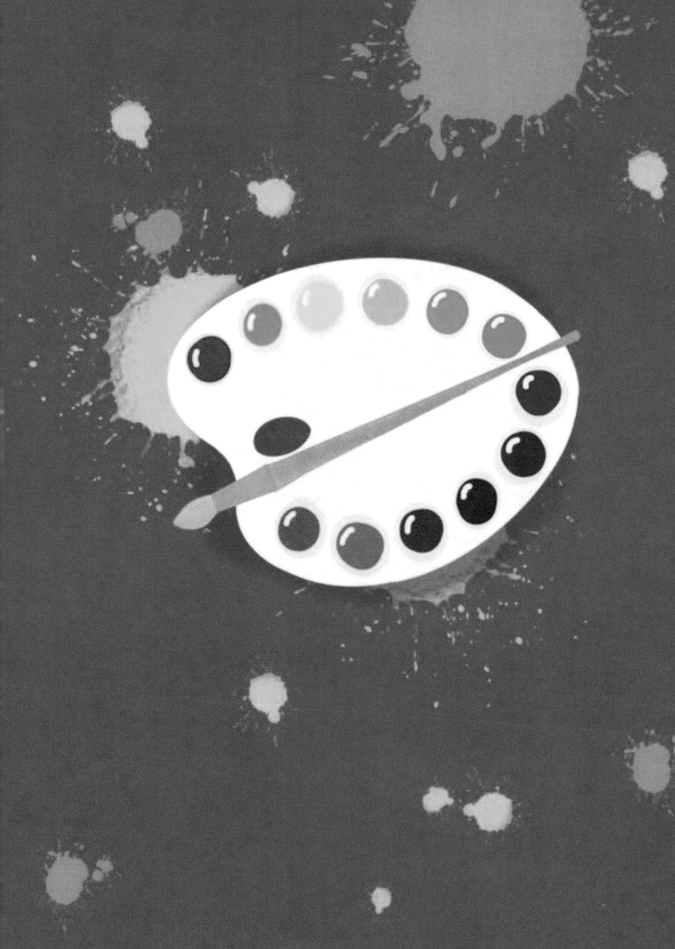

Hi, my name is Rosie!

I am eight years old. I have bright red hair.
I am short, and I love to draw.

I am in the second grade, and my teacher's name is Miss Martin.
She is very fun, and *very* good at spelling.
I hope I am as good as her at spelling long words when I'm old.

My best friend's name is Emily. She is in my class, but
Miss Martin says we can't sit together anymore
because we laugh too much.

It's okay, though. I still get to play with Emily at recess!

After school, my mom picks me up.
She drives a green car. We call it Froggy.
Sometimes, we even make funny frog noises.

I don't have a sister or a brother, but mommy says one day I might.

Lately, mommy has had a strange look on her face.
She thinks I have been peeing too much.
My daddy says it's normal because I play a lot, so I drink a lot of water.

Why is mommy worried about me peeing anyway?

Sometimes, I feel angry for no reason. It doesn't make sense to me.

Sometimes, I am playing and feel weird, like I want to take a nap.

I don't even like naps!

Naps are for little kids and I'm in the second grade...

I've been in second grade since fall. It's almost spring now.
Soon I will be in third grade.

In fall, I didn't know how to spell autumn, but now that it's a new year,
I can spell it better than anyone else in my class. I have been practicing.
A-U-T-U-M-N. Autumn!

Miss Martin is very proud of me.

I can't wait to see the tulips in our front yard again now that
spring is almost here!

Winter is sad.

There is a lot of snow, and I can't play outside as much.
I want to see the sunshine again.

Miss Martin has a weird look on her face
like mommy now. I don't know why.

I am still feeling funny... not in a good way.
Funnier than before. I feel bad.

I feel sadder. Mommy says I look like I lost weight.

I don't feel good.

Sometimes, I am really hungry and angry at the same time.

Last night, I wet the bed.
I cried a lot about it, but mommy said not to worry.

I wonder if daddy is worried. Grown-ups worry a lot.

Mommy made a doctor appointment for me on Wednesday.
I don't want to go. Doctors make me feel funny too.

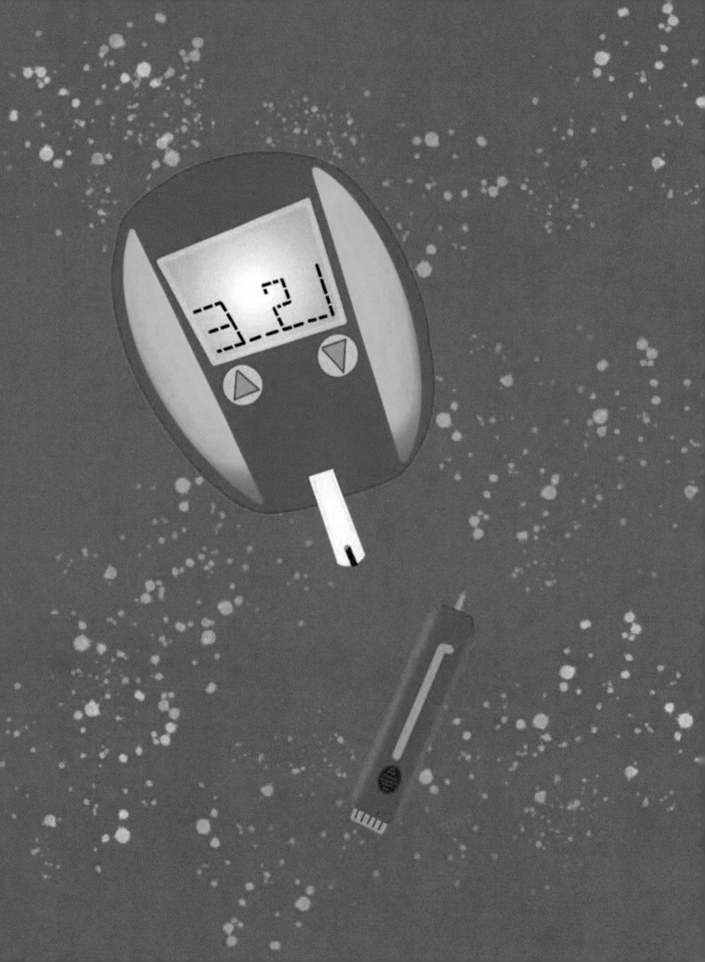

At the doctor, I had to sit a long time in the waiting room.
That made me feel worse. I don't like to wait.
I just want to go draw in the art room at school and play with my friends.

Mommy and I had to go into a tiny room
where the doctor stuck a sharp thing in my finger.
Blood came out when he did that.

He said he needed to test my blood.
Mommy said the sharp thing was a lancing device.

I will have to learn how to spell that so I can impress Miss Martin again!

It took a little while for the doctor to come back.
I was nervous because I didn't study for this test.
When he came back, he had the same look on his face as mommy.

I only get that look when I can't remember how
to spell a word on one of Miss Martin's spelling tests.

"What's wrong?" I asked.

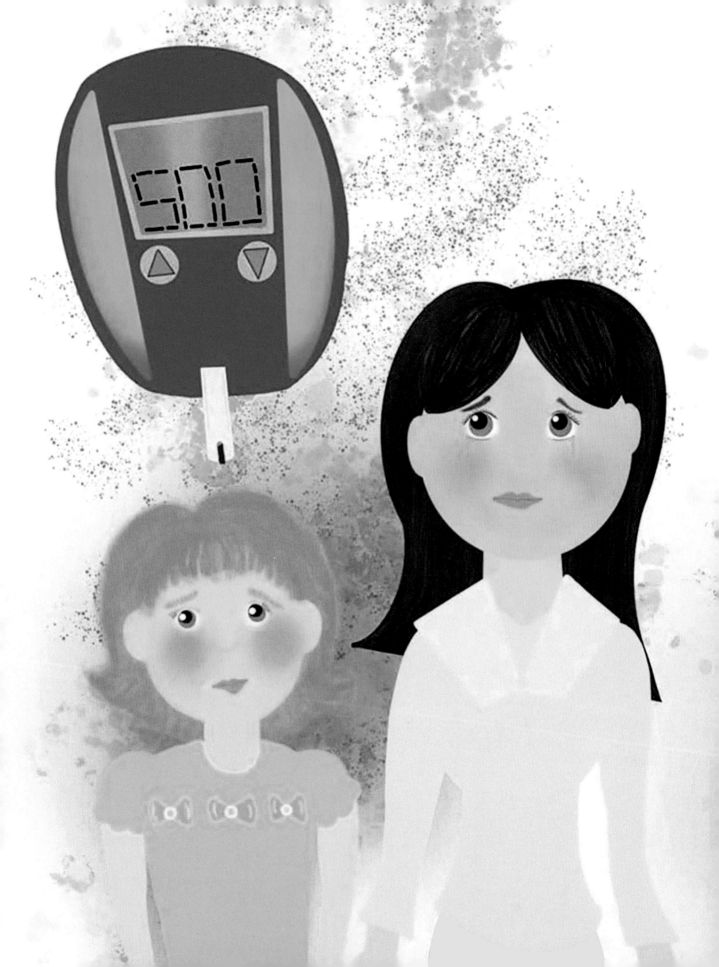

The doctor and mommy looked at me.

The doctor told my mommy I have something called type 1 diabetes and had to go to the hospital right away.

He said my blood sugar was 500.

I don't know what that is, but if 100 is good on a test,
500 has to be really good, *right*?

Mommy started to cry. That scared me.
I never saw mommy cry.

I didn't know what was going on.

Maybe 500 was bad…

Mommy called daddy, and he came to pick us up.
He gave me a big hug, but no ice cream.
Usually, when I have to go to the doctor,
he brings me an ice cream treat after.

I was sad I didn't get a treat. Maybe I did something wrong…

"Daddy, am I in trouble?" I asked.

"No, sweetheart. No, you're not," he said.

"Then why didn't I get an ice cream?"

"Well, honey. It turns out you have a condition called type 1 diabetes and your sugar levels are way off, so if I give you ice cream right now, it might make you feel worse," he said.

I did not like the sound of this…

"Will I ever get some again?"

"I'm not sure, honey. We will find out at the hospital."

First, hospitals.

Then, no ice cream?!

Plus, no art class?!?!

This was the worst day of my entire life.

I sat in the back seat of Froggy and started to cry.
I held onto my butterfly blanket for good luck. Good thing I left it there.

I hoped after this was all done I could go to
DeeDee's Ice Cream Shop with my parents again.

That is the best place in the whole world to get ice cream.

They are the only shop I know that has blueberry blast ice cream -
my favorite!

When I got to the hospital, I had to go into
a bright white room and put on a gown.

I laid in the bed, and then some nurses came in with a bunch of stuff.

They told me they had to hook me up to something called an IV.

A big needle came at me, and I got a little nervous.
The nurse said not to worry, though,
and that she would give me a reward after it was done.

That made me feel a little better. I became Brave Rosie for a minute.

"Good job!" she said.

"Thanks!" I said. I smiled at her. I wondered what my reward was.

She came back with a big stuffed animal.

This made the day better. *For sure!*

"A zebra?!" I shouted. I was not expecting that...

"Yes! This is Penny the Zebra, and her stripes are special," she said. "Do you see the sequins on her black stripes?"

I nodded.

The nurse smiled.

"You see, when you brush the sequins back, if it turns into a colorful spot, then that is where you can give insulin shots on your own body," she said, showing me how it works. "The doctor will tell you all about insulin shots later, Rosie. Remember, Penny is just like you."

"I'm not a stuffed animal," I said, confused.

She laughed and patted my head. If that was a joke, I didn't get it.

After the nurse put the IV in me and I watched cartoons on the TV in the room,
I started to feel a little better and went to sleep.

That night, mommy slept in a little bed on the floor next to me,
and daddy slept in a chair on the other side of the room.

There weren't many sleeping options at the hospital.
I wished I was in my bed at home.

In the morning, when I got up, the nurse came to check on me again.
She said my blood sugars were going in the right direction.
I still didn't know what that meant, but she seemed happy about it.

"Dr. H will come visit you later today, and explain more
about what's happening to your body," she said.

I nodded, a little nervous. On her way out, mommy
met her at the door and they talked for a while.

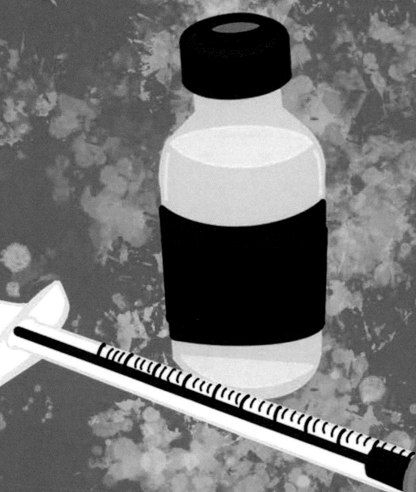

The morning went by fast. I wondered what Emily was doing at school...
probably playing with the Haileys on the playground.

I missed my friends.

Later on, the doctor came into the room.
He said hello to me and told me we needed to chat.

"Hi Rosie," he said. "I'm Dr. H. Are you confused about why you're here?"

I nodded.

"That's okay," he said. "I'm here to clear things up.
Well, Rosie, as you know, you have something called type 1 diabetes.

And what that means is, as I've explained to your mom
and dad, is that your body doesn't work quite like the rest
of the people you might know.

Most bodies produce something called insulin. Insulin helps our
bodies keep our blood sugar levels within a good range. Our blood
sugar levels need to be in a good range so that we feel good and are healthy.

Unfortunately, your body is not producing insulin like it should,
so you need a little help. Does that make sense so far?"

"Mmm.... I think so," I said.

"Okay," he smiled. "Rosie, what you will need to do now, with your
parents' help, is take insulin shots. This helps you be healthier, so
while you're here at the hospital, we're going to show you how to do
these shots so that you can be the healthiest and happiest when you
leave. How does that sound?"

"Okay, I guess..." I said.

The doctor showed me how to do the shots on an orange.
It looked pretty easy. Mommy tried it. Daddy did too.

They handed the orange to me and asked me if I wanted to try.

I did.

"Great job!" Dr. H said.

"I'm good at it?" I asked.

"You sure are! Maybe tomorrow, we can try it on you?
Do you think that would be okay?"

I thought about it. I looked at Penny the Zebra and
remembered what the nurse told me about her stripes.

"Yeah... I got this!" I said.

Brave Rosie was ready! I still didn't know about the ice cream yet,
but I felt better that Dr. H said I was doing a good job.

Maybe I could still get blueberry blast ice cream
at DeeDee's when we could finally leave here.

Rosie's Guide to T1D

GOALS

CARB CHART

INSULIN

The next day, I tried my first insulin shot on myself.
Mommy offered to do it for me, but I said I wanted
to be Brave Rosie, so I did it.

That was the first time I saw mommy smile since we got there.
I really knew I was doing good then...

The insulin shot stung a little, but Dr. H said that didn't surprise him
because I am tiny and need to gain some weight back.

The doctor and nurses taught me a bunch of math tricks that I had to use to
make my blood sugars good. They gave me a big book with everything
written down so that mommy, daddy, and I would never forget.

I found out I was going to have to take shots whenever I ate food from now
on, sometimes even when I wasn't eating food. And I would have to use my
lancing device to test my blood too.

If my blood sugar was high, the doctor said I might need to "correct it"
with insulin, even when I'm not eating. He wrote that down too.
Boy, there was a lot to remember...

Dr. H said I might have to do this the rest of my life.
I didn't know what I thought of that.
Maybe the smart scientists in the world would change that one day.

I'm only in the second grade, after all.

After a few days of being at the hospital and studying with the
doctors and nurses about what my body was doing and how
I needed to take care of it with mommy and daddy now,
the doctor said I could go.

Even better, he said that so long as I knew how to count the
carbohydrates of my ice cream, I could still have it sometimes.

Yay!!!

Carbohydrates - there's another word I need to learn
to impress Miss Martin with.

K-A-R-

No, no!

C-A-R-B-O-D-

Ugh. It's okay. I will get it.

First, I have to conquer this insulin thing.
Being Brave Rosie is *a lot* of work...

I am
type 1
strong!

It's been a few weeks now since I was at the hospital.
When I came back to school, I told Emily what happened to me
and she was excited that she got to walk to the nurse with me
everyday before lunch.

We had plenty of time to laugh on the way!
(We had a lot better jokes than the hospital nurse.)

The school nurse helped me make sure I took enough insulin for my food,
even though I knew how to do it myself because of the math tricks Dr. H
taught me.

My classmates were nice to me when I came back from the hospital.
I told them all about the orange, the IV, Penny the Zebra, Dr. H., and
lancing devices.

I even told them about insulin! They were amazed.

It's not easy having type 1 diabetes, but mommy, daddy, and I are managing it.

Together, we are strong. *Type 1 strong!*
That's a phrase I learned from the big book that Dr. H gave us.

Dr. H told me about a group I could join in my town to meet other
people like me - The T1D Connection for Kids.

I went to a T1D Connection for Kids meeting with mommy,
and they made me feel like Brave Rosie!

I met a lot of kids like me at the meeting,
and one of the leaders of the group told me that I am a warrior.

I liked that.

Brave Rosie Warrior!

No - Rosie Warrior!!

No - Warrior Rosie!!!

That's it! ...yeah. Warrior Rosie.

It's been over a month since I was at the hospital,
and I am learning how to deal with high and low blood sugar readings.
Low means I need sugar. High means I need insulin.

Being "low" and "high" both feel bad. But, mommy says it's okay.
I am learning, and the more I learn, the better I will be at controlling
my blood sugar readings.

I haven't peed the bed since I got back either - *phew!*

(I only told Emily that secret, but it's okay - we're friends for life.
She won't tell the Haileys.)

Dr. H called daddy's phone one day and said
once I am a "professional" at my lancing device,
I can get something called a CGM*.

He said that makes things easier and nicer for people like me, and
I will get to wear it on my body all the time, if I want to.

Plus, I won't have to feel the sharp needle or draw my blood as much.
It will tell me my blood sugar readings all day long.

It sounded good to me!
I might even get something called an insulin pump one day.

*A CGM is a continuous glucose monitor.

Now it's springtime, and I *did* become a professional at the lancing device.

Dr. H gave me a CGM. I wear it on my arm! It is my warrior shield.
It does most of the work for me and tells me what my blood sugar is.

(That's *very* nice of it.)

Emily and I pretend it has super powers to beam us wherever we want to go -
we have a lot of fun at recess.

Even better, mommy and daddy invited Emily to go get ice cream with us
at DeeDee's Ice Cream Shop tonight. It's a great day for Warrior Rosie!

Mommy says DeeDee's sccop of the day is double chocolate fudge.
I'm not even mad that it's not my favorite flavor, blueberry blast.
I'm just happy to be out of the hospital, and I am getting two scoops
because I know how to count my carbohydrates and plan for
my nighttime insulin.

My nighttime insulin helps me make sure my blood sugar is okay
when I sleep so mommy, daddy, and I don't have to worry.

Plus, I finally learned how to spell carbohydrates.

C-A-R-B-O-H-Y-D-R-A-T-E-S

That is a tough one, but I know Miss Martin is very impressed.

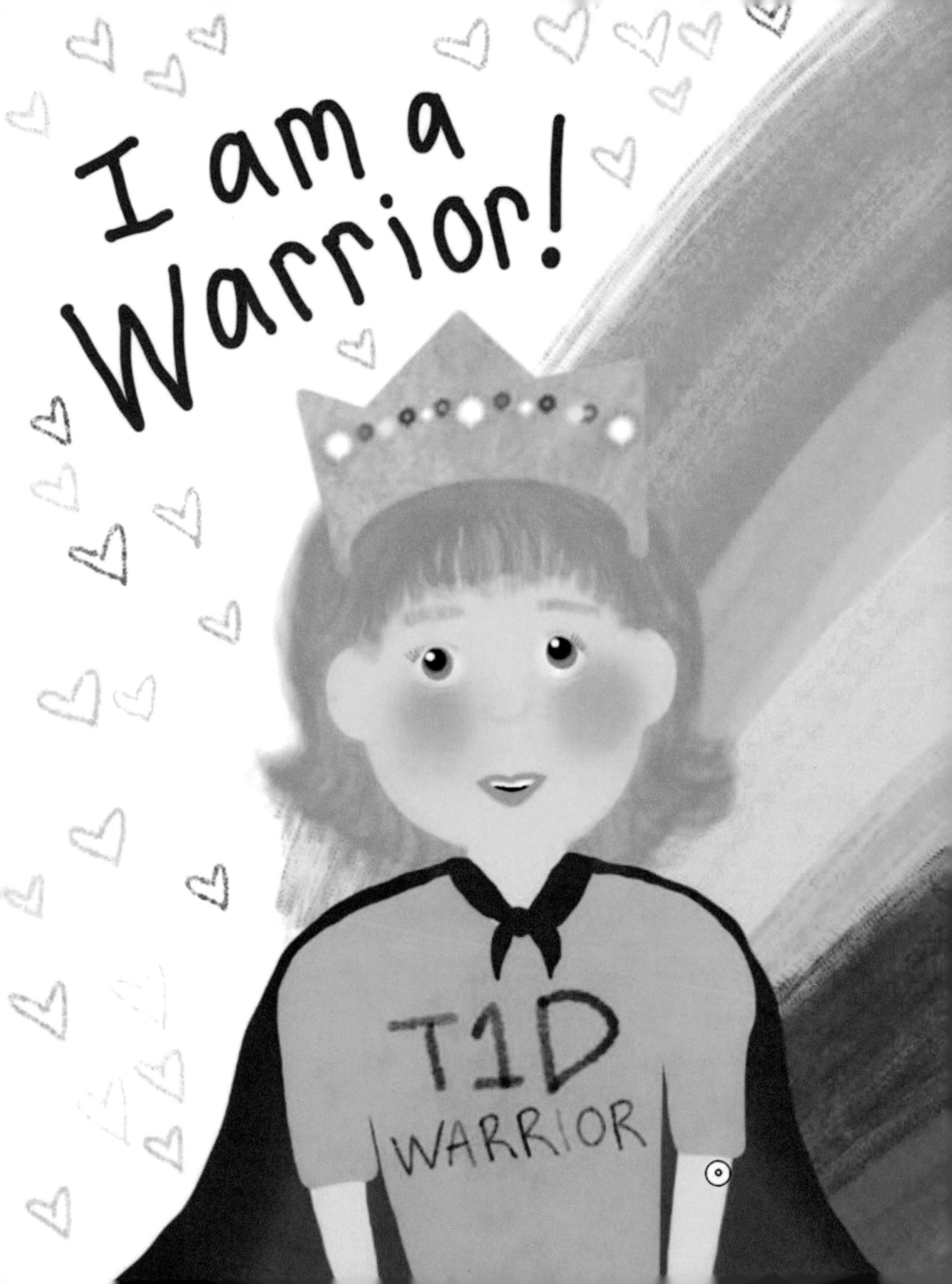
I am a Warrior!
T1D
WARRIOR

Second grade is almost done now.

I can't wait to be a third-grader.
Third-graders get to play outside later at night.

I think I will play a lot of flashlight-tag this summer.
I think I will win too - no one has super powers like me!

I have insulin. I have my CGM.
I have mommy, daddy, Miss Martin, Dr. H, and Emily.
I have DeeDee's ice cream, Penny the Zebra, my type 1 diabetes book, and my drawing books.

Dr. H said a lot of kids weren't like me, but it's okay -
not everybody gets to be a warrior.

I am ready to show the third grade Brave Warrior Rosie!

NOTES FROM THE AUTHOR

Hi, I'm Julia! As a type 1 diabetic of almost 20 years myself, I wanted to bring "Rosie the Warrior" to the T1D community to serve as a reminder that despite the highs and lows of this condition, a life with type 1 diabetes can be beautiful, full of laughter, happiness, and joy, and, most importantly - *you can be your own hero!*

Though living with a chronic illness can be serious, sometimes frustrating, and difficult, when you learn to manage it well, you can live a very fulfilling life and realize that, whatever you're going through, whether it be type 1 diabetes or something like it, the only limits you have are the ones you set for yourself. Rosie is for everyone, not just children with type 1 diabetes, though she was created with them in mind.

I want Rosie to serve as a reminder to all people that you are in charge of how empowered, happy, and confident you feel. Life is worth living and embracing with a youthful spirit.

For people with type 1 diabetes, especially, I want Rosie to remind you that you are capable of everything you want to be - type 1 diabetes or not.

For friends of people with T1D, I hope you develop a better understanding of your friends with T1D and learn more about ways you can be better friends to each other, supporting one another through all of life's highs and lows.

For parents, I hope you see your child in Rosie, and learn how to communicate with them more effectively about type 1 diabetes through her. I hope she provides a sense of comfort and understanding from the heart of your child with type 1 diabetes.

I hope Rosie brings a smile to your face, and perhaps - a reset for your perspective with the condition when you are most struggling. The highs and lows of type 1 diabetes are exhausting - such is life. Life is full of highs and lows, type 1 diabetes or not.

It's how we respond to and manage them that makes the greatest difference. Find opportunity and gratitude in difficulty for the lessons they teach you. Harness the positive energy and let the negative go. Life is too short to be anything but happy. I hope Rosie helps you live a little lighter and love yourself a little more, whatever you're going through, whoever you are, whatever your age.

Type 1 Strong,
Julia

READER DISCLOSURE

Made in the USA
Monee, IL
28 September 2021